Gumdrop
at the Zoo

Val Biro

Published by the Penguin Group
Penguin Books Ltd, 27 Wrights Lane, London
W8 5TZ, England
Penguin Books Australia Ltd, Ringwood,
Victoria, Australia
Penguin Books Canada Ltd, 10 Alcorn Avenue,
Toronto, Ontario, Canada M4V 3B2
Penguin Books (NZ) Ltd, 182-190 Wairau Road,
Auckland 10, New Zealand

Penguin Books Ltd, Registered Offices:
Harmondsworth, Middlesex, England

This edition first published in Great Britain in 1983
by Hodder and Stoughton

This edition published by Claremont Books,
an imprint of Godfrey Cavé Associates Limited,
42 Bloomsbury Street, London, WC1B 3QJ,
under licence from Val Biro, 1996

Printed in Italy

ISBN 1 854 71791 X

'Please take me to the Zoo today!' said young Dan to his Grandpa. It was a fine day and Mr Oldcastle felt like a drive in Gumdrop anyway. So he agreed.

'Hurry!' cried Dan. He liked going to the Zoo very much.

And Mr Oldcastle liked driving Gumdrop. He drove slowly round the roads of the Zoo until they reached a lake. There were many strange birds on the shore and Mr Oldcastle parked Gumdrop there for a while.

They walked over to a cage to see a large camel. He made some funny rumbling noises.
'I think he's got the tummyache,' said Dan. Mr Oldcastle agreed. 'And so would you if you ate two bales of hay for breakfast!'

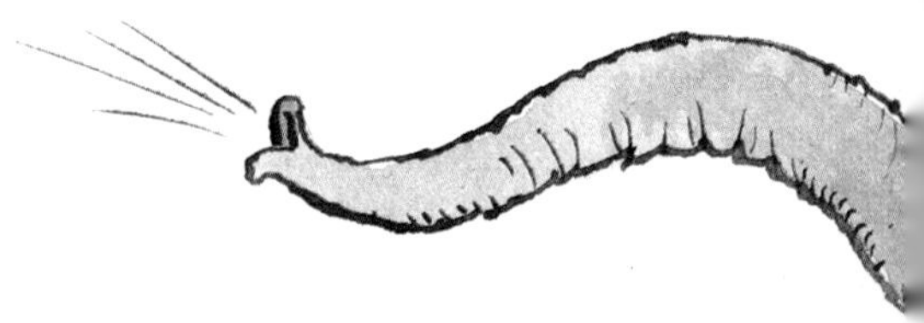

Next they saw an elephant. He made a sort of HONKY-TRUMPETY-HONK noise.

'Just like Gumdrop's horn!' said Dan.

Mr Oldcastle agreed but he began to worry about Gumdrop by the lake. 'I hope we won't find an elephant sitting on him!'

There was no elephant on Gumdrop, but he had birds all over him! There was even a little bay duck in the back.

'Don't shoo them away,' said Dan. 'I think they want to go for a ride.'

10

Round a corner they saw a notice which said:

The children who stood there looked miserable. So did the keeper, until he saw Gumdrop with the birds on top. He came hurrying over.

The birds took fright and flew away. Even the little bay duck in the back.

'Excuse me, sir,' said the keeper, 'but I see you give rides in your car. Now these children can't ride on the camel today because he has the tummyache. Would you please give them a ride instead?'

Mr Oldcastle agreed. The children cheered and jumped about.

'A ride in Gumdrop! Even better than a camel!' And the keeper changed the notice which now said:

Mr Oldcastle agreed and he drove carefully. People were amazed to see such a sight: a vintage car giving rides to a flock of birds! This must be a very special kind of Zoo, they thought.

PR 6719

They all had a ride. Gumdrop went right round the Zoo and every time they passed the elephant, Mr Oldcastle honked the horn. HONKETY-HONK. And each time the elephant replied: HONKY-TRUMPETY-HONK!

When it was time to go home, the Zoo Director thanked Mr Oldcastle and gave him free tickets to the Zoo.

Dan bounced for joy. ‘Now we can come back again tomorrow!’

But Mr Oldcastle was not so sure.

When they got home and cleaned Gumdrop, Dan found an egg on the back seat.

'Look! The little bay duck laid an egg in Gumdrop! She will want to sit on it so we MUST take it back tomorrow!'

And Mr Oldcastle agreed.